IRELAND

Madeline Donaldson

Lerner Publications Company • Minneapolis

To Maddie and Clare, who've got a good bit of the Irish in them

Lerner Publications Company
A division of Lerner Publishing Group, Inc.
241 First Avenue North
Minneapolis, MN 55401 U.S.A.

Website address: www.lernerbooks.com

Library of Congress Cataloging-in-Publication Data

Donaldson, Madeline.
    Ireland / by Madeline Donaldson.
        p.   cm. — (Country explorers)
    Includes index.
    ISBN 978–0–7613–6415–3 (lib. bdg. : alk. paper)
    1. Ireland—History—Juvenile literature. 2. Ireland—Social
life and customs—Juvenile literature. I. Title.
DA911.D66 2011
941.7—dc22   2010024221

Manufactured in the United States of America
1 – VI – 12/31/10

Table of Contents

Welcome!

You've just landed in Ireland! This island in northern Europe is part of the British Isles. The Republic of Ireland takes up most of Ireland. Northern Ireland isn't part of the republic. It is part of the nearby United Kingdom (UK). The UK also includes England, Scotland, and Wales.

Water splashes up on the shore of County Kerry in southwestern Ireland.

Water Inside and Out

Water surrounds Ireland. The Atlantic Ocean lies to the west, north, and south. The Irish Sea sits to the east. It separates Ireland from most of the UK.

The Cliffs of Moher in County Clare rise high above the Atlantic Ocean. County Clare is in west central Ireland.

Ireland has many lakes and rivers. The longest river is the Shannon. It flows southwest about 230 miles (370 kilometers). The Irish word for "lake" is *lough*. The Shannon travels through the loughs Allen, Ree, and Derg. It empties into the Atlantic Ocean.

Boats travel along the Shannon River in the town of Athlone.

Map Whiz Quiz

Take a look at the map on page 5. A map is a drawing or chart of a place. Trace the outline of Ireland on a sheet of paper. Can you find the Atlantic Ocean? Mark it with a *W* for west. Put an *E* for east by the Irish Sea. Color the Republic of Ireland green. Be sure to use a different color for Northern Ireland.

Low Mountains

Low mountains dot Ireland's western, southern, and eastern coasts. The Nephin and Connemara mountain ranges rise in western Ireland.

Cottages lie below the Nephin Mountains of western Ireland.

The Macgillycuddy's Reeks are reflected on Upper Lake.

In southern Ireland are the Macgillycuddy's Reeks, the Knockmealdown, and the Comeragh Mountains. The Wicklow Mountains lie in the east.

Rich Farmland

The center of Ireland is one big plain. Farmers have been raising crops and grazing livestock there for hundreds of years.

A farmer gathers hay during harvesttime.

Sheep eat grass in County Galway in central Ireland.

The main crops are potatoes and sugar beets.
Cattle and sheep munch on the plain's green grass.

The Emerald Isle

The greenness of Ireland comes from the large amount of rain that falls every year.

One of Ireland's nicknames is the Emerald Isle. Emeralds are bright green gemstones. And much of Ireland's land is covered in bright green grass.

The country has a mild climate. Summer temperatures hover around 60°F (16°C). Winter temperatures drop only to about 40°F (5°C). Snow is a rare event.

People use umbrellas during a short rainstorm. The rain doesn't stop them from shopping for flowers!

Long-Ago Ireland

People have lived in Ireland for thousands of years. One of the earliest groups to settle there was the Celts. They started ruling Ireland about seventeen hundred years ago.

The ruins of a Celtic castle stand on top of the Rock of Dunamase in central Ireland.

The Celts divided Ireland into kingdoms. At first, the Celts followed a nature-based religion. Over time, they accepted the Catholic religion.

The Story of Saint Patrick

Patrick is a famous Catholic saint, or holy person. Celtic sailors kidnapped Patrick from Wales when he was a boy. He spent several years in Ireland. During this time, he drew courage from his Catholic faith. He escaped and went back to Wales. There, he decided to become a priest. He returned to Ireland to teach religion to the Celts. Patrick included Celtic symbols—such as fire and the sun—in his teachings. This helped the Celts to accept the Catholic religion. Saint Patrick became the main saint of Ireland.

15

A statue of Saint Patrick stands at the base of Croagh Patrick, a mountain in County Mayo.

European Vikings attack Ireland in this artwork by Henry Payne.

Raiders and Invaders

Northern European Vikings began raiding Ireland about twelve hundred years ago. They robbed religious sites. But some Vikings decided to stay in Ireland. They set up some of the first towns, including Dublin, Cork, and Waterford.

The Normans from France came next. They invaded Ireland in the 1100s. They also ruled England. Over time, Norman-English kings ruled Ireland too. In the 1500s, England became a Protestant kingdom. English kings took land away from Irish Catholics. They wouldn't let Catholics practice their religion or speak Irish. These actions angered the Irish. They wanted the English to leave Ireland.

The ruins of Roche Castle from an English invasion in the 1600s stand in County Louth in northeastern Ireland.

The Great Hunger

Potatoes had long been a major crop in Ireland. Potatoes fed most of the island's poor people. But in the 1840s, a disease ruined the potato crop. People began to starve to death. More than a million Irish people died. That period was called the Great Hunger.

This drawing shows a starving Irish family during the Great Hunger of the 1840s.

Millions of Irish chose to leave Ireland during the Great Hunger. Many traveled to the United States and Canada. The Irish culture took firm root in many U.S. and Canadian cities.

In this image from the *Illustrated London News*, Irish people leave on ships bound for the United States.

Modern Ireland

Throughout the 1800s and early 1900s, the Irish fought to get free of English rule. By 1921, they had reached this goal—sort of. Most of Ireland became the Irish Free State.

During the Irish War of Independence (1919–1921), a shop in Cork was burned to the ground.

In 1949, the country renamed itself the Republic of Ireland. But the northeastern part stayed tied to England. It became part of the United Kingdom of Great Britain and Northern Ireland.

President Sean T. O'Kelly *(center)* signs the Republic of Ireland Bill in Dublin on December 21, 1948. The Prime Minister *(left)* and Minister for External Affairs *(right)* look on.

Who's Irish?

Most Irish have Celtic, Norman, and English roots. The people are known as warm and welcoming. Musical skill and clever storytelling are highly valued.

People walk along a busy street in Dublin, Ireland.

Since the late 1990s, newcomers from Eastern Europe, India, and Nigeria have moved to Ireland. Most are seeking jobs.

These people came from Romania to live in Ireland.

Old Language

Irish (sometimes called Gaelic) is one of Ireland's national languages. English is the other major language. The use of Irish almost died out under English rule.

These traffic signs are written in both Irish and English.

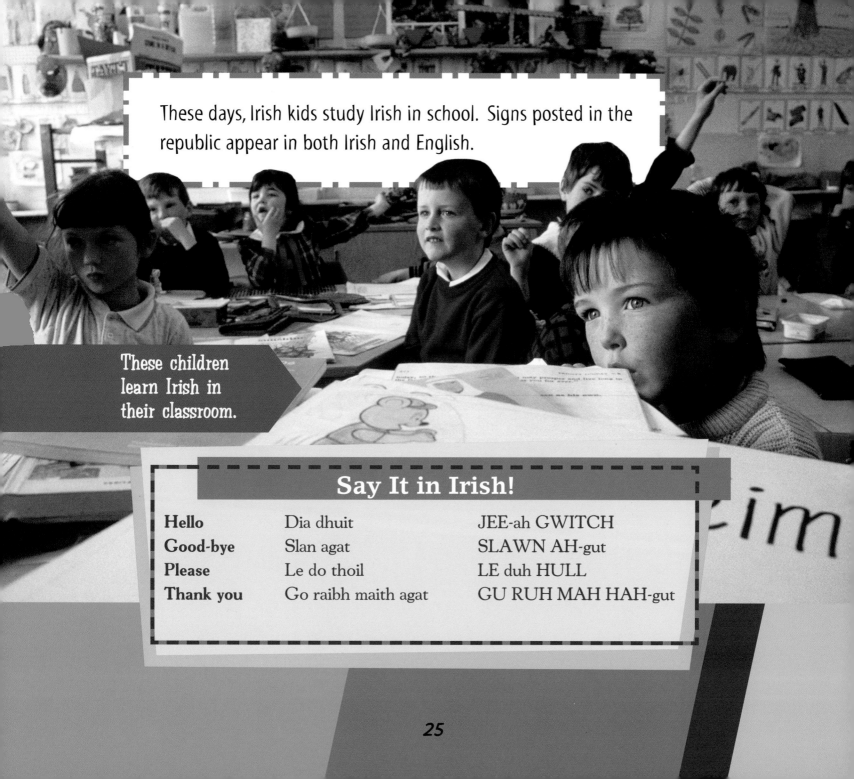

These days, Irish kids study Irish in school. Signs posted in the republic appear in both Irish and English.

These children learn Irish in their classroom.

Say It in Irish!

Hello	Dia dhuit	JEE-ah GWITCH
Good-bye	Slan agat	SLAWN AH-gut
Please	Le do thoil	LE duh HULL
Thank you	Go raibh maith agat	GU RUH MAH HAH-gut

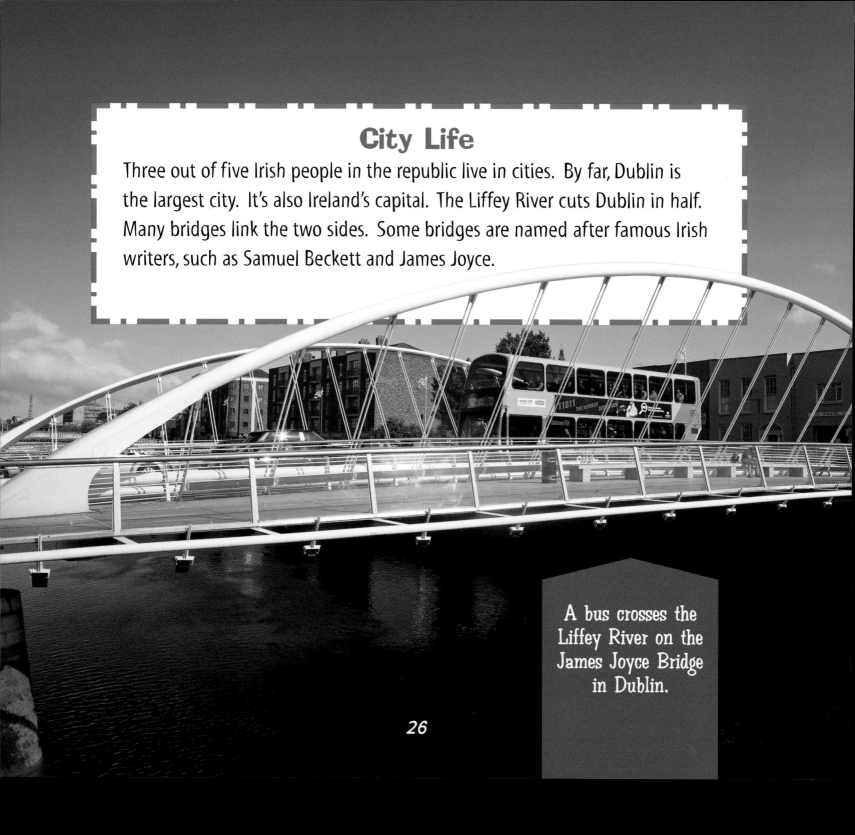

City Life

Three out of five Irish people in the republic live in cities. By far, Dublin is the largest city. It's also Ireland's capital. The Liffey River cuts Dublin in half. Many bridges link the two sides. Some bridges are named after famous Irish writers, such as Samuel Beckett and James Joyce.

A bus crosses the Liffey River on the James Joyce Bridge in Dublin.

26

Some other Irish cities include Cork, Limerick, and Waterford. Cork is a shipping hub in the south. Waterford, also in the south, is famous for glassmaking. Limerick lies in the west. It hosts many large businesses.

Cork

Dear Aunt Mary,

We're in Cork. Nearby is Blarney Castle, where I kissed the Blarney Stone. To kiss the stone, you hang over backward! You magically get the gift of gab in return. That means I'll be able to sweet-talk you out of your famous cookies!

Love,
Laura

27

Country Life

Two out of five Irish people live in the countryside. Some homes are small cottages with thatched roofs. Sheep and cattle graze on much of the land.

Sheep graze beside a home with a thatched roof.

Many small towns and villages feature people who make traditional crafts. These may include jewelry, pottery, woolen goods, and basketry.

This man wears an Irish sweater while working at Blarney Woolen Mills in County Cork.

Religion and Holidays

Most Irish people are Roman Catholics. A small number are Protestants. Irish Christians celebrate Easter and Christmas.

Christmas wreathes line the outside of a shop in Cork.

March 17 is another holiday. This is Saint Patrick's Day.

Dancers participate in the Saint Patrick's Day Parade in Dublin.

Schooling

Irish kids go to school from the age of four to the age of fifteen. Girls and boys usually go to separate schools. English is the main language.

These girls are wearing their school uniforms.

Kids study math, science, social studies, music, religion, and Irish. Most schools require kids to wear uniforms.

Students listen to their teacher during music class.

Sports

Most Irish people love sports. Hurling and Gaelic football are Irish favorites. But rugby, soccer, and golf are also popular. Irish teams have competed in hurling for nearly two thousand years. The girls' game is called *camogie*. Hurling and camogie are a bit like field hockey.

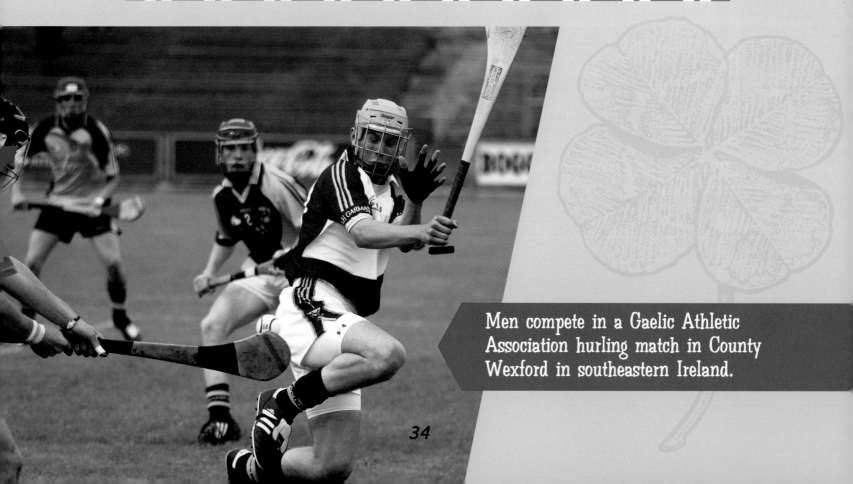

Men compete in a Gaelic Athletic Association hurling match in County Wexford in southeastern Ireland.

34

Gaelic football mixes some rules of soccer, rugby, and U.S. football. Players can touch the ball, but they can't pick it up from the ground. They can kick it or carry it. But they can't throw it. Players score points by kicking the ball into a net or through two goalposts.

Let's Eat!

Potatoes are common in Irish cooking. Cooks use them in stews, soups, and breads. They also serve them with lamb or beef.

This family eats breakfast together in southwest Ireland before the All Ireland championships in Irish dancing.

36

Salmon, caught in the seas near the island, are a specialty. Cheeses, such as Irish cheddar and Dubliner, are well known within and outside of Ireland.

A customer samples cheese at a market.

Irish Folklore

The Irish love a good story as much as they do a good storyteller. Most Irish folktales are shared by word of mouth. Some of the most famous stories feature leprechauns. These wee folk are said to have lived in Ireland before the Celts.

One thing leprechauns do in Irish folktales is repair shoes.

Fairies are also popular in Irish stories. Many different types of fairies exist. Banshees are fairies who cry loudly when an Irish person dies. *Sidhe* are tall, beautiful fairies who guard the forests.

Banshee fairies *(right)* often wear a cape. A giant named Finn McCool *(below)* is another common figure in Irish stories.

Finn McCool

Legends say the Irish giant Finn McCool sleeps in a cave beneath Dublin. He will wake up when Ireland most needs a brave warrior.

A man plays Irish folk music with a Celtic harp.

Tap Your Feet!

Irish music often gets folks clapping and tapping. The high-pitched tin whistle can have a cheerful or a sad sound. Classical Irish music groups might feature the Celtic harp, the Irish bagpipes, the flute, and the fiddle.

Players of Celtic drums hold the instruments, called bodhrans, on their side. The players beat out a deep sound with a hand and a drumstick.

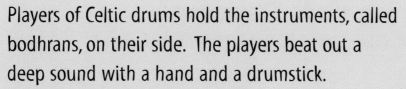

Irish Invasion

Irish music is popular worldwide. Famous musical artists from Ireland include the Chieftains, Van Morrison, U2, and Enya.

The popular Irish band the Chieftains perform.

Irish Folk Dancing

People of all ages take part in Irish dancing. This form of dancing is very old. It helped to keep Irish culture alive under English rule.

Irish dancers perform on Saint Patrick's Day.

Irish folk dancers move their feet quickly. At the same time, their upper bodies stay still. The dresses female dancers wear are decorated with Celtic designs. Ireland hosts world championships in Irish folk dancing every spring.

These girls' legs fly into the air during a dance performance.

43

THE FLAG OF IRELAND

Ireland's flag has three vertical bands of equal width. The bands are green, white, and orange. Green stands for the Roman Catholics in Ireland. Orange stands for the Protestants. The white band between the other two is for hope that the two groups will live in peace. This form of the flag became official in 1937.

FAST FACTS

FULL COUNTRY NAME: Republic of Ireland

AREA: 27,135 square miles (70,279 square kilometers), or slightly smaller than the state of South Carolina

MAIN LANDFORMS: coastal mountains, central plain

MAJOR RIVERS: Shannon, Liffey

ANIMALS AND THEIR HABITATS: red foxes, badgers, red deer, and viviparous lizards (throughout Ireland); porpoises and dolphins (oceans surrounding Ireland)

CAPITAL CITY: Dublin

OFFICIAL LANGUAGES: Irish and English

POPULATION: about 4.2 million

GLOSSARY

culture: the lifeways, including stories, music, and dance, of a people

goods: things to sell

lough: the Irish word for "lake"

map: a drawing or a chart of all or part of Earth or the sky

mountain: a part of Earth's surface that rises high into the sky

plain: a large area of flat land

saint: a holy person

symbol: something that stands for something else

thatched: straw-covered

TO LEARN MORE

BOOKS

Bunting, Eve. *Finn McCool and the Great Fish.* Ann Arbor, MI: Sleeping Bear Press, 2010. This story tells how the giant Finn McCool got his great wisdom.

Knudsen, Shannon. *Fairies and Elves.* Minneapolis: Lerner Publications Company, 2010. This book talks about the role of fairies and elves in folklore and myths.

Limke, Jeff. *Tristan & Isolde: The Warrior and the Princess.* Minneapolis: Graphic Universe, 2008. This graphic novel tells the story of the Irish princess Isolde. She marries an English king but forever loves the knight Tristan.

WEBSITES

Enchanted Learning
http://www.enchantedlearning.com/europe/ireland/index.shtml
This site has pages to label and color of Ireland and its flag.

Time for Kids
http://www.timeforkids.com/TFK/teachers/aw/ns/main/0,28132,1721735,00.html
This general site has a section on Ireland that includes a quiz, pictures, and a timeline.

INDEX